Kitten Castle

by Mel Friedman and Ellen Weiss
Illustrated by Lynn Adams

The Kane Press
New York

E
FRI

Book Design/Art Direction: Roberta Pressel

Library of Congress Cataloging-in-Publication Data

Friedman, Mel.
     Kitten castle/Mel Friedman and Ellen Weiss; illustrated by Lynn Adams.
        p.   cm. — (Math matters.)
     Summary: Anna uses household objects to build a structure to keep her cat's newborn kittens from getting underfoot.
        ISBN 1-57565-103-3 (pbk. : alk. paper)
        [1. Cats—Fiction. 2. Animals—Infancy—Fiction. 3. Shapes—Fiction.]
     I. Weiss, Ellen, 1949. II. Adams, Lynn (Lynn Joan), ill. III. Title. IV. Series.
     PZ7.F89775 Ki 2001
     [E]—dc21
                                                                                  00-043820
                                                                                  CIP
                                                                                  AC

10 9 8 7 6 5 4 3 2 1

First published in the United States of America in 2001 by The Kane Press.
Printed in Hong Kong.

Anna raced home after soccer practice on Saturday morning.

"Did it happen?" she asked her mom.

"See for yourself," Mrs. Cole said with a grin.

Anna dashed into the den. There, off in a corner, lay Streaks, the family cat. And nestled beside her were four tiny new kittens.

"Happy Birthday, kitties!" Anna said.

At dinner, Anna asked her parents the Big Question. "Can we keep the kittens?"

"Maybe," said Mrs. Cole.

"Maybe not," said Mr. Cole. "We have five goldfish, two hamsters, one canary—plus Streaks. Aren't nine pets enough?"

"Oh, pleeease, Daddy," Anna begged. "I'll take good care of them."

Mr. Cole thought for a while. "Okay," he said slowly. "They can stay. But only if they don't get in the way."

The kittens grew cuter every day. One had a chocolate coat. Anna named her Fudge. She was a cuddly kitten who liked to curl up in curvy places. Fudge hated corners.

Another kitten was a big climber. He liked to scramble up onto Anna's toy chest and sit at the edge. When the other kittens went by, he'd pounce!

"He's Ambush," Anna declared.

"He's a big pain," Mr. Cole said.

The third kitten had the sweetest face. Anna decided to call her Lovely.

Lovely was fussy about her toys. She only liked to play with things that rolled. So Anna gave her three roly toys.

The fourth kitten liked to tear around the house knocking things over. He'd disappear for hours, then turn up in the oddest places.

"That kitten is trouble," Mr. Cole said. And that's how Trouble got his name.

One morning Ambush woke Mr. Cole by
jumping on his chest.

Then Fudge tried to curl up in Mr. Cole's
wastebasket and knocked it over.

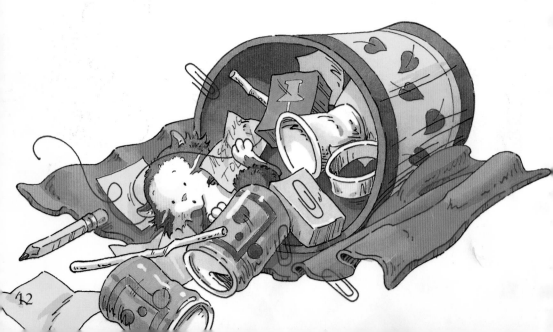

Next, Lovely found a new toy that rolled—
Mr. Cole's favorite pen.

And Trouble? He slipped into Mr. Cole's
closet and pulled down all his ties. Then
he fell asleep in a shoe.

"That's it," said Mr. Cole. "These kittens must go!"

"Give them just one more chance," Anna begged.

Mr. Cole sighed. "Okay," he said. "I go away on business tomorrow. We'll decide when I get back."

The next day Anna phoned her best
friend, Tom. "Come over quick!" she said.
"You've got to help me save the kittens."
Then she told him all about her problem.

Tom came right over. "Okay," he said. "Your dad doesn't mind the other pets, right?"

"They never bother him," Anna said. "The hamster stays in his cage. The goldfish is in his bowl—"

"Exactly!" Tom said. "We need to make the kittens a place of their own!"

"Of course," Anna said. "We can use boxes and put in lots of things the kittens will like."

"We can make it look cool, too," Tom said.

Anna pointed at a storybook. "Like a castle!" she said.

"We'll need boxes, tape, string…" Tom
said.

"And paint and markers," said Anna.
"Let's search the house!"

They kept on going until suppertime.

Tom was at Anna's first thing in the morning.

"Let's give each kitten its own special room," said Anna.

Lovely's box was first. They made it extra lovely, with bright colors and a fancy drawbridge. But Lovely wouldn't go in.

19

Anna had an idea. She put Lovely's roly
toys inside. "Now it's really her home,"
she said.

Lovely thought so, too. She ran inside
and started rolling her funnel.

Fudge's room was next. Anna and Tom put a large box next to Lovely's and painted it. But when they put Fudge inside, she jumped right out.

"I'll bet it's too boxy," Anna said.

"Huh?" said Tom.

"Fudge likes curvy places," explained
Anna. "Not square ones with corners."

"Well, how about that hatbox?" Tom
said. "It's round."

So they switched boxes. Right away,
Fudge hopped in and curled up. "Home
sweet home number two," Anna said.

The next day was Friday. Mr. Cole would be back Saturday!

"We'd better hurry and do Ambush's room," Anna said. "He needs a tall box so he can jump off it."

They stacked their tallest box on top of Fudge's. Ambush was in pounce heaven.

"One room to go," said Anna.

"What kind of room would Trouble like?" asked Tom. "Curvy? Square? High? Low?"

"Who knows?" Anna said. "Trouble is full of surprises."

They gave Trouble a nice room on the second floor with a toy mouse inside. "All the kittens like toy mice," Anna said.

They put in more cat toys and little pillows for naps. They added towers, pointy tops, and flags. The castle looked amazing!

"Here, kittens!" called Anna. "We're done!"

All the kittens came—except Trouble.

Anna and Tom called Trouble.
They looked for Trouble.
They put snacks out for Trouble.
But Trouble didn't come.

Anna's father got home Saturday morning. Trouble was still missing. But all Mr. Cole noticed was the peace and quiet.

"What happened?" he said. "There are no lamps crashing or kittens underfoot."

"Just follow us, Daddy," Anna said.

Anna and Tom led Mr. Cole into the den.

"Anna!" Mr. Cole said. "This is great!"

"It's a castle," said Tom.

"A Kitten Castle," said Anna.

"Where's Trouble?" Mr. Cole asked.

"We can't find him," said Anna.

All of a sudden they heard a noise coming from the hall closet. A little mewing noise. Anna opened the door. "Trouble!" she said. "There you are!"

Mr. Cole started to laugh. "So that's where that old shoe was. Maybe it should be Trouble's," he said.

"You mean, we can keep the kittens?" Anna asked.

"Yes," said Mr. Cole with a big grin.

And so, Trouble—and his shoe—moved into the Kitten Castle.

After that, Trouble wasn't trouble anymore—at least not when he was sleeping!

3-D SHAPES CHART

You can describe shapes in many ways.

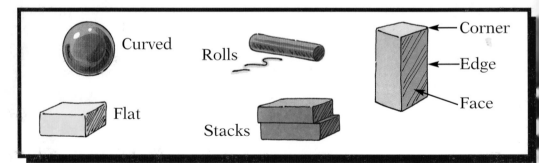

Curved

Rolls

Flat

Stacks

Corner

Edge

Face

Shape	Curved or Flat?	Rolls or Stacks?	How Many Faces?	How Many Corners?	How Many Edges?
rectangular prism	flat	stacks	6	8	12
cube	flat	stacks	6	8	12
cylinder	curved and flat	rolls and stacks	3	0	2
sphere	curved	rolls	0	0	0

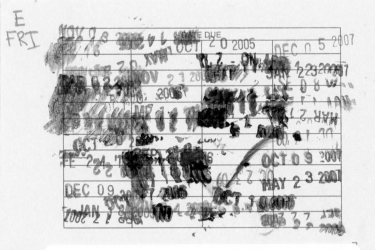